Animal Media Group books may be ordered
through booksellers, or by contacting:

Animal Media Group
100 1st Ave suite 1100
Pittsburgh, PA 15222
www.animalmediagroup.com
(412) 566-5656

Gina From Siberia
Copyright © 2018 by Animal Media Group

ISBN: 978-1-947895-00-3 (pbk)
ISBN: 978-1-947895-01-0 (ebk)
0422/B1861/A7
Printed in China

TO THE MAMAS AND PAPAS ALL OVER THE WORLD WHO SACRIFICE SO MUCH TO MAKE A BETTER LIFE FOR THEIR CHILDREN

WRITTEN BY
JANE BERNSTEIN
CHARLOTTE GLYNN

ILLUSTRATED BY
ANNA DESNITSKAYA

GINA from SIBERIA

When Gina was a puppy, she lived in a far-off land called Siberia with her family—Mama, Papa, Paul, and baby Danny. The winters were very long and snow fell every day.

Gina loved her home. She loved playing in the snow. She loved her apartment, which had six beds where she could sleep, and a laundry pile deep as a snow drift.

She loved Mama's food: kashka, smetanka, seledochka, kostochka. She loved her Babushka and Dedushka and her cousins, Zena, Yelena, Galina, Boris, and Irina. And of course, she loved her best friend, Gaidar, who lived downstairs.

Every morning, Gaidar would bark, and Gina would stand at the door until Mama, Papa, Babushka, or Dedushka took her out into the pine forest. Sometimes she and Gaidar played in the deep piles of snow for hours.

When Gina heard her parents say the family had to move, she was confused. Why would anyone leave such a wonderful place? Gina whined and barked. She sang, "Why, why, why?" She jumped high. She played dead.

Mama said, "You will be so happy in your new home."
"I won't," Gina said. She decided to stay unhappy forever.

Forever was going to be a very long time, Gina knew.
America was 5,681 miles away. Or maybe 5,682.

So many long train rides, so many long long lines.
Mama said, "Sooner than you know, we'll be at our new home."

When at last they got to the front of yet another long line, the ticket seller
rose from his stool and peered out the hole of his window at Gina.

"No dogs allowed on the train," he said. Gina worried she had asked "why" one too many times.

Would her family move to their new home without her?

A tall woman scooped Gina into her arms. "What a pretty little dog," she said. "I'll give you good money for her. With me, she'll have a very fine home."

Gina did not want a very fine home. She wanted to live with her family.
Mama said, "She is not for sale!"

Mama had an idea.

The train arrived. A conductor helped Papa lift the stroller and suitcases and bags.

Gina nervously watched the two conductors walking down the aisle, punching tickets. Mama whispered, "Ssssshhhhh. You must not make a sound."

Gina did not wiggle or whine or ask why.

One conductor looked right into her face. "What an ugly Russian baby," he muttered to his friend.

When Gina knew that her mama and papa loved her, she forgot her decision to stay unhappy.

There was so much to see on their long journey!
She saw a man with a beard down to his waist, eating soup with a small silver spoon.
She saw a woman dressed as a fox.
Dogs with tiny legs.
A boy with a ring in his nose sang a love song in the middle of the street.
Mama wiped her eyes.

She saw fleas hop high into the air.
She saw the ocean. Her paws left perfect prints in the sand.
Way up in the sky, geese flew in a perfect *V* and honked a sad song.
Papa wiped his eyes.
She tasted cocoa, whipped cream, egg noodle, and apple strudel.
Spaghetti, spumoni, macaroni, and baloney.

(25)

Finally, they boarded a plane that would carry them across the ocean.
Night turned into day, and when they landed, they were in New York City.

Nina, Marina, Ilya, and Dina were waiting at the airport, one crying harder than the next.

Nina lifted Gina into the air and said, "She looks like a boot!"

Marina drove them to their new home. Baby Inna pulled Gina's ears, and Lena squeezed her nose. Gina showed off her strong Russian teeth, and Mama said, "Gina, no!"

On her first day in the United States, Gina learned a lot. A traffic jam was something you sat in . . .

Jam was something you ate on toast.

Her new apartment had two beds . . . and no laundry pile.
Against the wall was a hissing monster.

Another monster lived beneath the street. It rumbled and screeched as if it were hungry for small dogs. Gina did not want to go outside and be eaten by this monster.

Gina spent long hours on the fire escape. Horns honked and big trucks squeezed past double-parked cars. Men rode on the backs of garbage trucks. Dogs played on the sidewalk. One big dog often looked up at her and barked hello, but Gina always turned away.

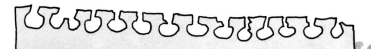

DEAR GAIDAR...

HERE I AM IN AMERICA.
I AM 5,681 MILES FROM
HOME. OR MAYBE 5,682.
THE SNOW IS GRAY.
THE OTHER DOGS SOUND
FUNNY. WISH YOU WERE
HERE.

 GINA

One day Gina stepped onto the fire escape and smelled something wonderful. Down below, a group of dogs was having fun on the sidewalk. Gina was tired of being lonely.

She stepped carefully down the fire escape. One flight. Another. Another. Another. And another.

The big dog ran over, his small tail wagging. "My name is Victor." He turned in a circle. "You're different," he said. "You're very small."

"My name is Gina," Gina said. "I was named after Gina Lollobrigida, the most beautiful actress in the world."

I'M FROM SIBERIA. OUR SNOW IS WHITE, AND TALL PILES ARE EVERYWHERE. YOU ARE VERY BIG. WHERE ARE YOU FROM?

THE BEST CITY IN THE WORLD!

REALLY? WHERE IS THAT?

RIGHT HERE!

I DON'T THINK SO. NAME ONE GOOD THING ABOUT THIS CITY.

WELL... WE HAVE MORE TO SMELL THAN ANYWHERE ELSE. AND ALSO THE BEST STREET FOOD. LET ME SHOW YOU AROUND.

As they strolled down Broadway, Gina told Victor about her cousins
Zena, Yelena, Galina, Boris, and Irina. Victor told Gina about his brothers
Ernesto, Claude, and Joe.

Gina told Victor about Gaidar, and Victor told Gina about his friend
Roberto. "He was named after the best baseball player in the world."

Suddenly, Victor darted away. He returned a moment later with something in his mouth for Gina. It was a slice of pizza.

She wolfed it down. "You do have the best street food," she said.

"I like you," Victor said.
"I like you too," said Gina.

Maybe it wasn't so terrible here after all,
Gina decided. Just different.

In the Soviet Union, life for Jewish people was very difficult. Many hesitated to practice their religion or celebrate holidays. Employers often refused to promote Jewish workers. In many schools, Jewish children felt unsafe and had to deal with discrimination. Sometimes, all that these children knew about Judaism was what they heard from playmates: being Jewish was not desirable -- or even acceptable. In order to keep their children safe, parents often didn't tell their children they were Jewish.

One winter, in 1978, an actual family—Mila, Joseph, Paul (11 years old), Danny (18 months old), and a miniature wirehaired fox terrier named Gina—embarked on a very, very long journey to leave the Soviet Union. They hoped to settle in the United States, where they would be free to live as Jews. On a train from Austria to Rome, they really did dress Gina as a baby so the guards wouldn't take her. HIAS, the Hebrew Immigrant Aid Society, helped the Backer family settle in New York. There they learned about Jewish culture and traditions and were welcomed into a community of families proud of being Jewish.